The Outlaw Robin Hood

JULIAN ATTERTON

Illustrations by

JOHN DILLOW

WALKER BOOKS

AND SUBSIDIARIES

LONDON • BOSTON • SYDNEY

CONTENTS

Robin Hood and the Miller's Son

Robin Hood and Little John

ROBIN HOOD
AND
THE MILLER'S SON

1 Forest Law

Long ago, in the kingdom of England, there lived a man named Robin Hood.

One morning in May he looked at his fields and told himself that little needed doing until the hay was ready to cut, so he called to his ploughman, Will Scarlet, and together they set out into the greenwood.

The trees were uncurling new leaves, and from their branches came the song of birds flying north again after the winter. Robin and Will walked deep into the forest, where the trees grew tall over their heads and the path narrowed to a deer-track through an undergrowth of hazels and thorns.

They each carried a longbow of polished yew and a quiver of arrows, and as soon as they reached an open glade they stopped to

set strings to their bows, then each notched
an arrow between the string and shaft.

"Set me a target," said Robin. "As high and
far as you like."

"You sound sure of yourself," said Will. "I
would like to see you hit the dead branch on
that oak over by the thicket of brambles."

Robin raised his bow, and a moment later his
arrow struck the branch with a force that made
it crack and fall to the ground.

"Your eyes are sharp this morning," said Will.

"My eyes are as keen as my heart," said

Robin with a laugh. "Marian has told me she loves me."

"Ah," said Will. "That tells me why you asked for a high and far target. Half the girls in the village have you in their hearts, and there you are losing yours to the one maiden in the parish who will be hard to win. What of her father, old Sir Gilbert? He strikes me as the kind of knight who is too proud to let his daughter marry a farmer."

"We shall see," said Robin. "Tonight I am to dine with him."

They were startled from their talk by a noise in the forest. They heard undergrowth being trampled by a beast moving fast and carelessly, then a long drawn-out bellow and a cracking of branches.

"A stag," said Robin. "In pain, by the sound of it."

"Aye," said Will, "and I can hear men giving chase."

"But no hounds or horses," said Robin. "I find it hard to believe that the lord de Lacy has taken to hunting on foot."

"We had best take cover," said Will. "With bows in our hands we look all too much like men out hunting deer, and we both know what the lord de Lacy does to those he catches poaching in his forest."

As they ducked into the undergrowth, they saw a stag canter into the centre of the glade only to fall to the ground and lie still. Running after it came two youths in simple country clothes, and as one of them bent down to pull out the arrow that had brought the beast its

death, Robin and Will recognized one of their neighbours, Much the Miller's son.

"Do you see who I see?" whispered Robin.

"Aye," said Will, "and the other lad is young Dickon."

"They ought to know better," said Robin, but as he spoke he grinned. "Shall we pay them our respects?"

Springing from the bushes, Robin and Will walked out into the glade, whistling as if they just happened to be passing by.

"Well met, neighbours," cried Robin. "It is a fair morning to be out in the greenwood."

Much and Dickon spun round to stare at Robin and Will with eyes full of guilt and surprise.

"You make a lot of noise when you go hunting," said Robin. "Count yourselves lucky we are not foresters."

Much took a moment to find his tongue.

"We are lucky it is you," he agreed. "You do not look the kind of men who go telling tales."

"No, we tell no tales," said Robin. "But I think you fools to steal from the lord de Lacy. Have you no wits? Surely you know how cruel he can be in the name of upholding the law?"

Much met Robin's gaze with a smile that curled bitterly, like the ripple made by a stone thrown into a well of anger.

"Oh, I know the law," said Much. "I learnt it last winter when my father died. He was still unburied when the lord de Lacy sent his steward to take away the best of our animals, and then I had to pay a fine for the right to work my father's mill. I was told that was the law, but it left me with so little I hardly know how to feed my mother and sisters until the harvest."

Robin reached into his belt-pouch and gave Much all the coins he had with him.

"Take this to your mother as a gift," he said, "and may you get safely home. Will and I will be on our way and leave you to your luck."

Robin and Will strode on, and had soon left the poachers far behind, but their steps were no longer so carefree. Silently they turned and made for a lane that ran through the forest and gave the quickest way back to the village. They had taken hardly ten steps from the trees when riding towards them they saw a knight in fine clothes, and six leather-clad men-at-arms.

"It may no longer be enough," muttered Robin, "to leave friends to their luck."

Raising his hunting-horn to his lips, he blew
two sharp notes as a warning to Much and
Dickon to stay deep amongst the trees. The
men-at-arms gripped their weapons in surprise,
and a moment later Robin and Will found
themselves surrounded by the horsemen.

The knight leaned forward in his saddle and
studied their faces.

"Why do you sound your horn at our
approach?" he asked.

"Surely a brave knight deserves a peal of

greeting?" asked Robin. "I trust you are indeed a brave knight, for you hardly need to be with such a large escort to protect you."

The knight's face hardened into a cold and haughty mask.

"I am Sir Guy of Gisburn," he said, "steward to my lord de Lacy. Are you his men?"

"Nay," said Robin. "We hold our land free. I am Robin Hood, and my friend is Will Scarlet."

"Never again let me hear your horn in my lord's forest," said Sir Guy, speaking slowly and grimly. "You might be mistaken for poachers."

"As you see," said Robin, "we have nothing to hide."

"God help you if ever you have," said Sir Guy, "for no one else will." And with that he rode on, followed by his men-at-arms.

Robin drew a long breath and turned to Will.

"There goes a man," he said, "who I would hate to have against me."

"All I know," said Will, "is that if that is how you set about making friends, I would rather not be with you on a day when you want to make enemies."

2 Riders in the Night

That evening Robin went to dine with Marian and her father, Sir Gilbert Fitzwalter.

Sir Gilbert was a knight who, after years of serving his lord, had been rewarded with a piece of land to call his own, though after a life spent in castles he knew nothing of farming. His son had died fighting for the king, and because of this he loved his daughter as if she were the last treasure he possessed.

Robin found it hard to enjoy his meal, but once the trestle-tables had been cleared away, Sir Gilbert stretched his legs and began to talk.

"I will make no secret of thinking Marian a maiden worthy of a knight," he said. "But sadly it seems that these days the noble knights ride away on crusade, and only the narrow-hearted stay at home. You are a good man, Robin, and I judge from all Marian has told me that she will never love another the way she loves you."

"For my part," said Robin, "I know I will never be happy unless I am worthy of her love."

Sir Gilbert reached out and clasped both Robin and Marian by the hand.

"I give you my blessing," he said. "And I say we should call for the cup of betrothal."

So Robin and Marian drank in turn from a cup inlaid with silver, and stared deep into each other's eyes as they drank.

"I have an old friend who is a priest in Pontefract," said Sir Gilbert. "Perhaps we should go and visit him?"

As he spoke there was a clattering of hooves along the lane that ran past the house, and Sir Gilbert rose quickly to throw open a shutter and stare out into the gathering dusk.

"An ill wind," he murmured. "Sir Guy of Gisburn and his pack of wolves in armour, and I doubt they are out merry-making." He turned to Robin. "Sir Guy was here not long before you came, telling me a stag has been poached from the forest, and bidding me tell him if I hear of any venison being sold."

Robin said nothing, but to Marian, who was watching him, it seemed that the joy had gone out of his face. As Sir Gilbert closed the shutter, Robin rose to his feet.

"The night has come too quickly," he said, "so let me thank you for your kindness and take my leave."

"So soon?" asked Sir Gilbert. "I trust you will dine with us again tomorrow."

"Nothing could keep me away," said Robin, and turning to Marian he raised her hands to his lips. "How can I sleep when you are in my thoughts?" he asked her. "Your eyes are darker than the leaves of the copper beech."

"Your words," said Marian with a smile, "are richer than the pie we ate for supper."

Reaching the wooded lane, Robin turned for a last glimpse of Marian as she stood waving from her doorway, but the moment he was out of sight Robin took to his heels and ran like the wind. He did not stop until he had passed through the village and come to the cottage by the beck where Dickon lived with his family.

All was peaceful, and a twist of blue hearthsmoke was curling out through a hatch in the roof. Knocking on the door, Robin walked inside to find the family at supper.

"Welcome, neighbour Robin," said Dickon's father. "Join us for a cup of ale."

"Nay, though I thank you," said Robin, "I come only to speak with Dickon, and beg you spare him from the table for a while."

As soon as they were outside, Robin shook Dickon by the shoulders.

"Sir Guy knows there has been poaching," he said. "What did you do with the stag?"

"Have no fear," said Dickon. "We sold it to a butcher from Pontefract."

"Does he know you by name?" asked Robin.

"Aye," said Dickon, "we have sold him a stag once before."

"Then he may have betrayed you," said Robin. "I have just seen Sir Guy and his men riding at a gallop."

Dickon struggled to twist free of Robin's grip. "Let me go," he said. "I must warn Much."

"Use your head," said Robin. "That is the last thing you must do. I will warn Much. You must take to the woods and hide. Come to my farm at daybreak."

Leaving Dickon to gather his wits, Robin ran

on down the path beside the beck. As he reached the head of the mill pond he heard the barking of dogs and the snorting of horses, and at the mill itself he found the men-at-arms dragging Much from his hearth while his mother stood screaming at them from the doorway.

"You treat that man too harshly," cried Robin, and as the men-at-arms turned in surprise he found himself face to face with Guy of Gisburn.

"Well met, Robin Hood," said Sir Guy. "I trust this is the man you tried to save by blowing your horn?"

"Leave him be," cried Much. "He had no part in it."

"Silence," ordered Sir Guy. He gave a signal at which Much was thrown onto one of the horses and tied across the saddle.

"If you had no part in this," he asked Robin, "why are you here?"

"To beg you for mercy," said Robin. "When the Miller died you took his animals in the name of the lord de Lacy. Much's only crime was to try and feed his family."

"He has broken the law," said Sir Guy.

"He has killed a stag," cried Robin, "and only because his family needed to live."

"He has broken the law," repeated Sir Guy, stepping up into his saddle. "The penalty for poaching is mutilation, the cutting away of left thumb and forefinger so the poacher may never again hold a bow. As custom demands, the sentence will be carried out on market day at Pontefract, so that all who see may be reminded of the law."

"Are you a knight or a demon?" cried Robin.

"I beg you, wait until the king's justice comes to Pontefract. Let me plead for my friend before the court."

"Enough," snapped Sir Guy. "My men will tell you what I think of the king's justice."

One of the men-at-arms struck Robin with his fist, then a second struck him with a force that knocked him to the ground. By the time he had struggled to his feet, the men-at-arms had mounted their horses and were ready to ride away, and Robin felt as if he were boiling with an anger he had never known before in his life.

"Sir Guy," he called. "What you are doing is cruel beyond justice, and I vow it will not go unpunished."

"The weak should never make threats," replied Sir Guy. "My men will mark your face in their minds, and if you are ever such a fool as to come to Pontefract, you may find it hard to leave alive."

And with that Sir Guy of Gisburn rode off with his escort of men-at-arms, carrying Much the Miller's son to the dungeons of the castle of Pontefract.

3 Marian

At dawn the next morning Robin's mother rose from her bed to find her son sitting like a ghost beside the ashes of the fire.

"You look as if you have had no sleep," she told him, and in answer he told her all that had happened the night before.

"Poor Robin," she said sadly. "You have set yourself a hard choice. You have made a vow to Sir Guy, and you have made a vow to Marian. You cannot keep them both."

"Why not?" asked Robin.

"If you strike against a knight as strong as Sir Guy," she said, "he will see to it that you lose either your land or your life. To lose either is also to lose Marian."

"Then what do you advise?" asked Robin.

"Look to your own hearth and harvest," said

his mother gently. "Leave it to God to give Sir Guy the judgement he deserves."

Robin gave deep thought to her words, but the end of it was that he looked up and shook his head. "I will leave Sir Guy to God," he said, "but I cannot leave Much to Sir Guy."

"And can you leave Marian?" asked his mother.

"Nay," he answered. "That I could not bear."

Robin went outside to wash and, as he splashed himself at the trough, he saw Dickon walking towards him from the trees. With him was Will Scarlet.

"You are making a name for yourself," said Will. "The whole village is talking of the words that passed between you and Sir Guy last night."

Robin gave a groan. "Soon they will be talking about the difference between words and deeds," he answered.

"Not if we can help it," said Will. "For at the moment all that matters is that market day in Pontefract is not until tomorrow. We still have a day and a night to find a way of saving Much."

"You would risk coming with me?" Robin asked him. "Sir Guy will be waiting with a wolf-pack of men-at-arms. By sunset tomorrow we could either be outlaws or dead."

"Aye," said Will, "but if we stand together we can shoot arrows so fast they will think we are wizards from Lapland."

"And you, Dickon?" asked Robin. "What do you say?"

"I say we go," answered Dickon. "Last night I had a taste of running away. I think I would rather live my life full of fear but staring ahead than full of fear and always looking over my shoulder."

"So tell us," Will asked Robin, "are you our leader?"

Robin avoided their eyes and gazed at his fields.

"I cannot answer until I have spoken with Marian," he said.

"Do whatever you think best," said Will, "but do not leave it too long."

Robin worked in the fields until well after noon, then he washed his face and hands, combed his hair and beard, and walked up the lane to the house of Sir Gilbert Fitzwalter.

Sir Gilbert gave him a good welcome and, while they were waiting for Marian to come

down from her chamber, he led Robin to a
wooden chest, and threw back the lid to reveal
his savings of gold and silver.

"I have not asked you what you want as a
marriage-gift," said Sir Gilbert. "Take whatever
you wish."

"Nay," said Robin. "You have already given
me your greatest treasure."

"Well said," replied Sir Gilbert. "For those
words I will give you the only other treasure I
possess."

He led Robin to a second wooden chest, but

this one he unlocked with a key that hung from his belt. Reaching inside, he drew out a sword in a scabbard of red leather and held it out to Robin.

"Take it," he said. "It was my son's."

Robin drew the sword from its scabbard and felt the weight of the blade.

"I have never seen so fine a weapon," he said. "Surely it has a name?"

"My son called it 'Dayfarer'," said Sir Gilbert, "for his vow was to draw it only in daylight, and to use it only with honour."

As he spoke, Marian came into the hall, her hair garlanded with flowers, and ran to Robin with arms outstretched.

"What you two need," said Sir Gilbert, "is a long walk in the orchard."

Once they were alone among the trees, Marian looked into Robin's eyes and frowned.

"What is it?" she asked. "Why are you so troubled?"

Robin told of the stag, and of Much, and of the vow he had made to Sir Guy.

"Do you believe Much can be saved?" asked Marian.

"I will never know unless I try," said Robin.

"Yet how can I risk losing the love I have found with you?"

"You must follow your heart," said Marian. "All I ask is that it brings you safely back to me."

"How can it if I am outlawed?" asked Robin.

Marian drew a long breath and took hold of Robin's hands.

"Outlaws can be pardoned," she said, "and men like Sir Guy of Gisburn fall from power when their masters grow tired of them. I will wait for you, Robin. I have no choice, for I will love you as long as I live."

As she spoke she gripped his hands so tightly that it seemed to Robin as if her strength were flowing into him.

"Have you any idea," asked Robin, "how I can get myself past the guards who will be watching at the gates of Pontefract?"

"They will be watching for a man in country clothes who carries a longbow," said Marian. "Are they likely to notice a well-dressed gallant, who rides behind my father in a wedding procession?"

4 Market Day

The town of Pontefract stood on a hill above
the valley of Aire, and on market day the streets
began to bustle at first light.

As the gates were thrown open by the guards,
the merchants threw open their shops.
Streaming through the gates came the farmers
and traders with goods to sell, and hard on their
heels were the folk from the villages around,
who came to meet, to gossip, and to buy.

At each gate stood one of Sir Guy's men-at-
arms, with orders to stay in the shadows, but to
make sure they were shadows that gave a good
view over the gate-keeper's shoulder into the
faces of all who stopped to pay their toll as they
passed into the town.

Watching the south gate was a man named
Gurth.

"Will you know the man you seek?" asked the gate-keeper.

"I ought to," said Gurth. "Two nights ago I threw my fist into his face on the orders of Sir Guy."

"And you think he will come back for more?" asked the gate-keeper.

Gurth only shrugged. "Most men take the message of a beating to heart," he said, "and never give trouble again. But this one picked himself up with anger in his eyes. Some wild horses take a lot of taming."

By the time the sun was high, the streets were crowded and Gurth had lost count of the faces he had searched without finding the one he sought. All of a sudden he caught sight of a tall, cloaked and hooded man, who was pausing to pay the gate-keeper. As the man reached for a coin from his belt-pouch, Gurth saw that beneath his cloak he gripped a stem of polished wood of about the same width as a longbow.

"You there!" cried Gurth. "Stand where you are!"

Stepping out of the shadows, Gurth laid hold of the man's hood and jerked it down onto his shoulders. What he saw made him catch his

breath, for the stranger had the build of a giant.
His face looked as if it had been hacked out of
stone. His beard was a thick tangle of curls, but
the crown of his head was bald and marked by
a long red scar which looked as if it had once
been a deep and wicked wound.

"So you remember me?" asked the giant.

"Nay," said Gurth. "Should I know you?"

"Only the Devil lets his servants forget their
crimes," said the giant. "I am John, the shepherd of Melton. On my head you see the mark
of the blow Sir Guy of Gisburn had me given
when my flock got in the way of his hunting."

"You hide a weapon," said Gurth. "Let it
fall."

John the giant threw back his cloak to reveal

a shepherd's crook of polished oak, which he raised to point to nine fat sheep that a dog was herding up the street towards the market. He gave Gurth a mocking look, and said nothing.

"Pass," said Gurth angrily and, as the giant moved on, Gurth found himself muttering a curse on Sir Guy for making him so many enemies.

He was still gathering his wits when he heard horses and a jingling of harness bells. Through the gateway rode an old knight, and behind him on a palfrey garlanded with flowers rode a maiden veiled in white. From her head-dress hung a trail of white silk, so long and wide that it fell in folds down the flanks of her horse.

She was followed by three horsemen, but Gurth barely saw them, for his eyes rested on the maiden and he turned to gaze after her as she rode on up the street. He watched until she had passed from sight, then turned with a sigh to guard the gate, never to know that he had just failed in his task. Had be but glanced at the man who rode behind the maiden he would have recognized Robin Hood.

Robin sat stiffly in his saddle, whispering thanks to the Mother of God once he knew the

gates were safely passed. He wanted to turn
and grin at Will and Dickon who rode behind,
and to call out words of love to Marian, but he
kept his lips tight and used his eyes to learn all
he could of the town.

The riders merged with the crowds in the
market-place, which was a meadow below the
gates of the lord de Lacy's castle. Half of it was
covered by stalls, where under brightly-
coloured awnings the merchants and traders

sold goods from the four corners of Christendom. The other half was crammed with wattle-fenced pens, where the butchers and farmers gathered to haggle over the price of livestock.

Gazing over the stalls, Robin saw that by the castle gate there was a hillock of trampled earth on which stood a row of whipping-posts, with iron rings for men to be tied to them.

Beside them burned a brazier, where a man-at-arms was heating branding-irons in the coals. It looked as if the law-breakers would soon be led out to suffer their punishment.

Sir Gilbert dismounted by a towered church, far older than the castle, that stood on a corner of the market-place.

"Wait here for me awhile," he told the others. "I will go and see if Father Maurice has had my message and made things ready for the ceremony."

As soon as he had gone, Marian turned her palfrey so she could sit watching the castle gate. At a signal from Robin, Will drew his horse up to her left, while Robin nudged his own to stand on her right. Children ran up to them to beg, and the townswomen on their way to

market stopped to wonder at Marian's finery,
and to call out blessings on the bride-to-be.

"I wish the sun would stand still," said
Marian.

"If only for an hour," said Robin. "All I ask is
the time for us to be wed, for to come so near
and not kiss at the altar would be too cruel."

"Aye, you deserve it," said Will. "You could
always tell the priest to hurry, and I will stand
by the door and give you a whistle when Sir
Guy slithers out of his hole."

"Too late," whispered Marian. "Look!"

Sir Guy was riding out of the castle gate on a

black charger whose ironshod hooves clattered on the timbers of the drawbridge. Behind him marched a squad of men-at-arms, and behind them, pale-faced from the dungeons, stumbled three men in torn and filthy clothes.

"Is Much among them?" asked Marian.

"The one in the middle," answered Robin. "You can tell him by his bandy legs."

Behind Much there marched a second squad of men-at-arms.

"By the beards of the Saints," muttered Will. "Look at the size of that guard! Sir Guy never takes things lightly."

They watched the procession stamp from the gate to the hillock.

"I count seventeen of them," said Robin breathlessly.

"More than enough," said Will, "but if I take six, and you take six, Dickon can have the other five. How many arrows did we bring?"

"Three quivers," whispered Robin, "with eight shafts in each."

"At this distance we may waste a few," said Will, "but there should be enough to go round. I say we chance it."

"Dickon?" asked Robin.

"Just give me a bow," said Dickon.

Robin and Will dropped from their saddles to the ground, and shielded by their horses from the gaze of passers-by, they lifted the folds of the silk train that hung over the haunches of Marian's palfrey. There, strapped below her saddle, hung their longbows and quivers of arrows.

"I leave you my arrows," said Robin, "and will trust to my sword and your marksmanship. Be ready for my signal when I reach the market-cross."

He reached up and helped Marian to dismount.

"My love," he said, "I beg you to take refuge in the church."

"Are you telling me to hide?" asked Marian angrily.

"Never," said Robin. "I am asking you to pray for me."

"God go with you, Robin," she answered. "I will pray for tomorrow's light."

As Marian hurried into the church, Robin heard her silk train rustling on the stone floor.

Then he walked as fast as he dared through the market, brushing past the good folk who

34

crowded round the stalls in a babble of bargaining. They were used to seeing justice done on market day, and when the criminals were paraded on the hillock above their heads, they lowered their eyes and bargained louder than ever, as if refusing to let Sir Guy spoil their morning.

Reaching the tall stone cross that was older than the castle, Robin sprang up the steps and set his back against the shaft. An alley of stalls was all that lay between him and the hillock, and he could hear the sergeant-at-arms crying out the laws that had been broken and the penalties that must be paid. He saw Much shivering with fear, and Sir Guy strutting around in a shining coat of chain-mail.

Sir Guy was watching the market, eagle-eyed, and he caught sight of Robin at once. They stared silently at each other along the alley of stalls, then Sir Guy smiled, a slow smile that hovered like a hawk preparing to strike.

Robin Hood raised his hunting-horn to his lips and blew a note so loud and clear that even the market-goers of Pontefract fell silent.

5 Trial by Combat

"Hear me, Guy of Gisburn," cried Robin. "You who call yourself a knight."

"Witless peasant," answered Sir Guy. "Have you come to be branded with the other rogues?"

"Nay," cried Robin. "I come to challenge you." And so saying, he drew Dayfarer from its scabbard and held it high so the sunlight was mirrored by the blade. "You seek to punish men by cruel and unjust laws," cried Robin. "I say they should go free, and I challenge you to meet me in single combat, man to man and blade to blade. Let God decide which of us is right."

Sir Guy turned lazily to his men-at-arms.

"Seize him," he ordered.

The men-at-arms sprang forward, but they

had hardly taken a pace when the air hummed and two of them fell, choking on the arrows in their throats. Sir Guy flinched as if he himself had been struck, and a moment later he and his men were leaping down the sides of the hillock towards the shelter of the stalls, while in the high bell-tower of the church, Will and Dickon bent their bows, and each arrow they loosed struck a man to the ground.

"Much," cried Robin, "save yourself and your friends. Horses are waiting by the door of the church."

He watched Much and his comrades scurry down the sides of the hillock and plunge into the maze of the market, then set his back squarely against the stone cross and turned to face the alley of stalls down which Sir Guy was running towards him with his pack of men-at-arms. The market filled with shrieks as the townsfolk drew back and mothers snatched their children out of the way, giving Will and Dickon so clear a view of their target that their arrows continued to rain from the sky.

Robin watched the men running to attack him fall one by one, but not all the arrows met their mark; and when he counted the last and knew that his friends' quivers were empty, there were still three men running towards him, and one of them was Sir Guy.

"Hold fast," cried Will from the bell-tower. "We are on our way."

Sir Guy was the first to reach the foot of the cross, and fixing his eyes on Robin he drew his sword. It was a longsword, with a blade so heavy that Sir Guy had to grip the hilt with both hands to lift it into the air, and he swung it at Robin with all his might.

Robin raised Dayfarer to meet it, and as steel clanged on steel the shock of the blow ran through his body like pain. Straining to keep his guard he thrust the blade away, but the effort left him so shaken he almost lost his footing.

"This is going to be like felling a tree," said Sir Guy. "Whichever way you fall one of my men is waiting to catch you on his sword."

"Mother of God," prayed Robin, "give me strength."

Just as Sir Guy was raising his sword to strike again, a hooded giant stepped out from among the stalls and thrust his way into the fight.

"The man called for single combat," he

roared, "and I say he deserves it."

With that he threw back his cloak and raised a stout shepherd's crook, bringing it down onto the head of one of Sir Guy's men-at-arms with a force that knocked the man senseless. His comrade sprang past Robin to lunge at the giant with his sword, but the giant turned swiftly and gave his attacker a blow with his

crook which lifted him off his feet and dropped him in the middle of a stall of pottery, which collapsed on top of him with a crash.

Robin watched in wonder, and saw the hooded giant turn to him and grin with crooked teeth that gleamed through a tangle of beard.

"There," said the giant. "Now the odds against you are even, my friend. Sir Guy of Gisburn is yours."

"The churchyards of England are full of men who speak too soon," said Sir Guy. "It will be a pleasure to kill you both."

He raised his longsword and swung it against Robin with a strength that came from his fury, and Robin knew at once that he could never withstand the blow. Lowering his guard he let the blade swing towards him, then at the last moment sprang sideways, so that instead of hacking into him, the longsword struck the stone shaft of the market-cross. Steel rang on stone, and the blade splintered into a hundred shards in a shock that made Sir Guy gasp and fall to his knees.

"You have him," roared the giant. "Quick, make an end of the beast."

But Robin bent down to pick up a sword dropped by one of the men-at-arms, and gripping it by the blade he offered it to the knight.

"Now, Sir Guy," he said softly, "let us fight with swords of the same weight, and may God be our judge."

Sir Guy swayed to his feet and took the weapon, but his gaze turned from Robin towards the church. Will and Dickon had run down from the tower and were galloping on horseback towards the market-cross. At the sight of them Sir Guy threw down his sword, turned, and ran towards the castle. The giant bellowed with laughter, and one of the townsfolk hurled a cabbage at the back of the fleeing knight.

"God be praised," shouted Will as he drew rein by the cross and saw that Robin was unharmed.

"Aye, and not only God," said Robin. He turned to thank the hooded giant, but the giant was nowhere to be seen.

"Strange," murmured Robin. "Where..."

"Hurry," said Will. "Once Sir Guy is safe in the castle he will raise the hue and cry, and if the gates are closed against us we are finished."

Gathering his wits, Robin sprang into the

saddle of his horse. Much leapt up behind him and all but broke Robin's ribs in a hug of thanks, while the other two men who had been rescued climbed up to ride behind Will and Dickon. Turning their horses they galloped out of the market, yelling to the townsfolk in the streets to make way.

Down by the south gate, Gurth was still on watch, but he had been filled with foreboding ever since his brush with the hooded giant. He heard whispers in the shadows, and every face he saw looked evil, so it was almost a relief when he heard shouts and galloping hooves, and turned to see horsemen racing for the gate. At their head rode Robin Hood with a sword in his hand.

The gate-keeper grabbed his takings and fled, leaving Gurth to break out in a sweat. He knew that if he moved fast he could bar the gate, but it would leave him no time to save himself.

"Come to think of it," he muttered, "it may be that Sir Guy is not a man I want to die for."

So he stood back, and closed his eyes to the dust kicked up by the hooves as the horse-men thundered past him and out into the countryside.

6 The Brotherhood

Once inside the castle Sir Guy called for men
and horses, prowling around like a hungry bear
while they made themselves ready. Seizing a
battle-axe from the armoury, he mounted the
first horse he found and galloped out down the
streets of Pontefract with a troop of thirty
armoured men hard on his heels.

As they rode out of the gate, they found Sir
Gilbert Fitzwalter waiting on horseback with a
drawn sword in his hand.

"I ask your help," he cried. "The knave
Robin Hood has dishonoured my daughter. He
led her to the altar only to leave her standing
there unwed and disgraced."

"Saw you which road he took?" asked Sir
Guy.

"I did," answered Sir Gilbert. "Follow me!"

Spurring his horse he galloped away, and Sir Guy and his men set their horses in pursuit. They rode long and hard, but they never set eyes on Robin Hood, for Sir Gilbert led them west towards Wakefield, knowing full well that Robin and his friends had taken the road that ran south, to Wentbridge.

Yet Robin and his friends knew none of this, and were riding south with grim determination, as with two men to a saddle their horses began to tire. Fear stayed with them until passing through Wentbridge they reached the cover of the wide woods of Barnsdale.

When night fell they were hidden in a glade in the depths of the forest, sitting around a fire of fallen branches watching Dickon turn the spit on which a wild boar was roasting over the flames. As darkness gathered in the trees the men fell silent, thinking of the hearths and loved ones they had left behind. Robin thought of Marian, and how nearly she had been his bride.

Will Scarlet broke the silence by slapping his knee.

"It has been such a full day," he said, "that it only strikes me now that I am sitting here among strangers. Much, you have not told us the names of your two comrades."

"I am Swain the Baker," said one of them.

"And I am Perkin the Fletcher," said the other.

"So," said Will, "a man who makes bread and a man who makes arrows. We will need you

both if we are to live out here in the wilds."

"Have we no choice?" asked Much.

"By now we will all be outlaws," said Will.
"To go back to our homes would bring danger
on our kin."

"I will never feel safe here in Barnsdale," said

Much. "We are still within the borders of the lord de Lacy's domain."

"Aye," said Will, "but a day's walk to the south and we can be in the forest of Sherwood. No one will want to hunt for us there. We can live on the king's deer and the travellers on the king's road."

"Not so fast," said Much. "I will be a poacher, but not a robber."

"I like it no more than you do," replied Will, "but it seems to me that if we want to stay alive we must stand together. I say we choose a leader, and I also say we must choose Robin."

There was a murmur of agreement, and Robin was torn from his thoughts of Marian by the knowledge that five pairs of eyes were watching him and waiting for an answer.

"I have no heart to lead a band of robbers," he said after a while, "but I will gladly share my fate with any man who joins me in taking a vow of purpose."

"Tell us what is in your mind," said Will.

"We will make the greenwood our domain," said Robin, "and we will charge a toll from any rich merchant or fat churchman who comes our way. But we must vow never to harm any

lady, or pilgrim, or good knight, or poor trav-
eller."

"That sets it fairly," agreed Will.

"There is more," said Robin. "We must vow
to go to the help of any good folk who find
themselves oppressed by the lords of the land,
even if in doing so we risk our lives the way we
risked them today."

"Amen," said Much gratefully.

"And lastly," said Robin, "we must vow to
live together as a brotherhood, and to be of
good cheer. Above all, let us leave our sorrows
behind and be merry."

And with that the companions joined hands
around the fire, and swore to be loyal to each
other until the day of their deaths.

It was a vow that was often to be tested in the
years that followed, by torture, by bribery, and
by doubt, but it was a vow that not one of them
ever broke. Bound together in fellowship, they
found a new life of freedom in the forest. There
were other men, with their own stories to tell,
who came to join them, and so began the chain
of adventures that were to make Robin Hood
and his brotherhood the most famous outlaws
in the kingdom.

Robin Hood
and
Little John

1 The Hooded Giant

In the heart of the forest of Barnsdale, the trees grew so thickly that their branches hung out over the highroad.

One summer morning, not long after day-break, the branches of a great elm rustled then were still, as into them climbed a young man dressed in green. From his belt hung a sword and a hunting-horn, and from his perch he looked out over the forest the way a lord looks over his domain; and there was nothing strange in that, for this man was none other than the outlaw, Robin Hood.

Before long he heard a distant sound of singing, and he soon caught sight of two monks journeying south along the road, leading a string of pack-mules whose baskets were stuffed to the brim and covered with sacking.

Robin waited until they neared the elm, then
he set his horn to his lips and blew a peal that
sent a hundred birds flying from the trees in
alarm. The monks froze in their sandals, but
before they had time to look up, Robin had
swung down through the branches and
dropped to the ground to face them.

"Greetings to you, my brothers," he said.
"May I ask where you are bound?"

The monks were too busy rolling their eyes

to reply, for at the call of Robin's horn, a dozen men had stepped out of the trees to surround the pack-train. Each was dressed in green, and they each carried a longbow of polished yew.

"Saints preserve us," said the elder monk. "Who are you and what do you want?"

"I am Robin Hood and these are my companions."

"Then we are as good as dead," sobbed the monk.

"Your thoughts are too dark for such a fair morning," said Robin. "I want your names, not your lives."

The monk took a deep breath and gathered his dignity.

"I am Brother Hubert," he replied, "and this is Brother Godfrey. We are white monks from the grange at Wentbridge, and we are taking our vegetables and cheeses to the brothers of Blyth Priory."

"Blyth Priory," exclaimed Robin. "I should have thought the monks there were rich enough to feed themselves."

"They would be, but for you," muttered young Brother Godfrey. He spoke under his breath, but not softly enough to pass unheard.

"And what do you mean by that?" Robin asked him.

The monk stared at his toes. "Blyth Priory has a guest-house for travellers on the high-road," he explained. "The brothers are always happy to shelter travellers for the night, but nowadays, whenever rich merchants hear that you and your robbers are in the neighbour-hood, they hide in the priory until they think you have moved on. They are eating the monks out of house and home."

Robin roared with laughter. "Far be it from me to steal the supper of men whose purses I hope to empty," he said. "Good brothers, I grant you the freedom of the forest, and the right to pass without paying a toll."

"May the Mother of God reward you," said Brother Hubert.

"I thank you for your blessing," said Robin, "and I trust you will remember that you owe me a favour."

He was still laughing as the monks hurried on, but his good cheer vanished when he saw that his companions were glaring at him.

"Have you lost your wits?" asked Will Scarlet. "What do you mean by letting a rich catch like that slip through our fingers?"

"Oh, come now," said Robin, "you know your-self that white monks are rich only in land and what they make of it."

"Even so," said Much the Miller's son, "I would have given anything for one of their cheeses."

"Or some crunchy carrots," murmured Dickon.

"The bitter truth," said Will Scarlet, "is that every time we strike we put ourselves in danger. We cannot afford to play at being high-handed and noble."

Robin's eyes narrowed. "Listen to me, all of you," he said. "We swore when we became brothers of the forest that we would never rob good men, and that is how it will be for as long as I am your leader. Are you tired of your vows?"

The outlaws fell silent, but their faces were sullen.

"Well, I have had enough of lurking by the roadside for one day," said Robin. "I suggest we go our separate ways, and meet again this evening at the Camp of the Squirrels. Let us hope that by then our tempers are on the mend."

With that he strode into the forest, hardly caring which path he took just as long as it led him deep into the wild places, where he could be alone with his thoughts.

"A curse on all this," he whispered. "A curse on Guy of Gisburn for driving me to outlawry, and keeping me away from Marian my love, and a curse on the cruel times in which we live."

Robin walked until his anger was cooled by the peace of the forest. Some hours later he was dozing against a tree when the distant sound of vesper bells told him it was time to turn back towards the clearing where the outlaws had their camp.

On his way homewards he came to a swift-flowing stream over which a tree trunk had been laid to serve as a bridge. As Robin stepped onto it, a giant of a man appeared out of the trees on the other bank, and without so much as a glance at Robin he stepped up onto the far end of the trunk.

"Not so fast, good fellow," cried Robin. "I was here before you, and I claim the right to cross first."

"Get out of my way, you dung-beetle,"

growled the giant, and he lumbered towards Robin so that they met in the middle of the bridge. Robin looked up at his opponent and shivered, for the giant wore a hood, and all that could be seen of his face in the evening shadows was a tangle of beard and a crooked row of teeth.

"It seems you need a lesson in courtesy," said Robin, and he thumped the giant in the chest. But the giant stood as solid as a rock, and before Robin could strike again he reached out with a huge hand and gave Robin a shove that sent him flying off the bridge into the stream.

Soaked and spluttering, Robin crawled up through the brambles and nettles of the riverbank to find the giant squatting on the ground, with his hands covering his face.

"That was not like me," said the giant. "Not like me at all."

Shaking his head sadly, he looked up at Robin, and after one good look at the giant's face, Robin gave a gasp of recognition.

"I know you," he exclaimed. "You came to my rescue in the market-place of Pontefract when I was fighting for my life against Guy of Gisburn and his men-at-arms."

"Aye, that was me," replied the giant. "I am glad to see you got away alive."

"And ever since I have been wishing we could meet again so I might thank you," said Robin. "Tell me your name."

"John of Melton," said the giant, but he spoke almost as if he were ashamed of the sound of it.

"And I am Robin Hood," said Robin, holding out his hand.

This time it was the giant who gasped. He eyed Robin from head to toe and gave a grim chuckle.

"Robin Hood," he repeated slowly. "That is a name I hear spoken with fear and trembling from Nottingham to Sherburn. And to think I nearly drowned you! I beg your pardon, great outlaw."

"And I will grant it, Little John," said Robin, "but only if tonight you eat supper with myself and my companions."

"Gladly," answered Little John, "for I no longer have a hearth of my own to go to."

"It sounds to me as if there is a tale in that," said Robin. "Perhaps you will tell it as we eat?"

2 The Giant's Tale

It was dark by the time Robin Hood and Little
John arrived in the clearing the outlaws called
the Camp of the Squirrels. The rest of the band
was there already, seated round a fire, and the
air was rich with a smell of simmering stew.

"So this is your home," remarked Little John.

"One of them," answered Robin. "We have
other camps over in Sherwood, for we never
like to stay long in one place."

As they walked towards the fire, Will Scarlet
sprang up to greet them.

"It is good to see you, Robin," he said.
"None of us are proud of the words that were
spoken this morning."

"This morning is forgotten," said Robin,
"and my wanderings have been rewarded, for I
have here the man who saved my life in the

market-place of Pontefract. Friends, I bid you make a place by the fire for Little John."

"No one could be more welcome," replied Will, "though I must say I cannot see what is little about him,"

"Let us hope it is not his appetite," said Robin.

Yet Robin was right, for when supper was served, Little John showed no hunger. The outlaws plied him with a thick stew of venison and lentils, and with fresh barley buns from Swain the Baker's turf-covered oven, and with a mellow ale that had been rescued from a merchant who was taking it to market in Pontefract; but Little John sipped and pecked as if none of it tasted good to him.

"By my faith," exclaimed Robin, "you have a small stomach for a man so huge."

"Take no offence if I make a poor guest," answered Little John. "The truth is simply that I care no longer for the fruits of this earth."

"So I see," said Robin. "You said when we met that you have no hearth to call your own. May I ask where you were bound when our paths crossed?"

"I was taking the first steps of a long

journey," said Little John. "I am bound for the Holy Land."

"A noble quest," said Robin, "yet a pilgrim needs to eat if he is to reach his goal."

Little John stared into the fire. "It hardly matters if I get there or not," he replied. "All I ask is to live long enough to shake the dust of England off my feet."

"There is a story hidden in your words," said Robin, "and I guess it to be one of injustice and suffering. Many tales have been told around

this fire, and if you wish to unlock your heart we will listen in silence."

Little John nodded thoughtfully, and ran his fingertips along a deep scar that marked the bald crown of his head. After a while he began to speak.

"It sometimes happens," he said, "that the happiness of those dear to him can mean more to a man than his own, and it goes by the same rule that their sorrows can break his heart. I was the shepherd of High Melton, and my master's daughter Clara was the apple of my eye. When she found love with a young knight named Adam, the sight of them together made my old heart creak with joy. They vowed to be married, but before it could come about, my master died and Clara was left an orphan."

Little John paused for a drink of ale.

"Now you all know the cruel law that says an heiress becomes the property of her overlord, and that is what happened to Clara. Earl William seized her and shut her up in his castle of Conisbrough. The law gives him the right to marry her to the man of his choice at the moment of his choice, and there the matter rests. Adam cannot help her, I cannot help her, and to tend my flocks within sight of the walls of Conisbrough is now more than I can bear."

"There is one thing in your tale that puzzles me," said Robin. "Amongst barons, Earl William has a name for being a just and honourable man."

"He may well be," said Little John, "but he spends most of the year on his lands in Sussex, leaving Conisbrough in the charge of a knight named Ernald of Mort. It is Ernald who seized Clara in the earl's name, and no one has ever mistaken Ernald for a just and honourable man."

Robin sat forward. "Then he deserves a poke in the eye," he said. "I say we go and free this maiden from her cage. Who comes with me?"

"Wait just a moment," begged Will Scarlet. "Have you ever seen the castle at Conisbrough? It has the highest walls and the tallest tower in the land."

"I am with you, Robin," said Much the Miller's son.

"And I," said Dickon; but the other outlaws, who were older and more wary, looked from Will to Robin, then back to Will, and Will gave a long, low groan.

"Oh, Robin," he said. "You ask the earth."

"That I know," said Robin, "yet when we first became brothers of the forest we vowed to use our strength to help those in need, even at the risk of our lives. I will ask no man to come with me on a venture he thinks is folly, and I have never been one for rash boasts over a cup of ale. Much, go and saddle me one of our horses. Tonight I have some riding to do."

"Where are you going?" asked Will.

"Never you mind," said Robin, "and never fear. I will be back by daybreak. Little John, I trust you will spend the night here as our guest?"

Little John nodded in some bewilderment as Much emerged from the trees leading the brotherhood's finest mount, a grey stallion fit for a king. Robin pulled on his gloves, patted the horse's neck, and swung himself up into the saddle.

"Take every care," begged Will. "I do not like this business."

Robin reached down and clasped his friend by the hand. "Nor do I like to think of Ernald of Mort breaking a maiden's heart," he said.

And with that he rode off into the night.

3 A Glimpse of the Prison

The streets of the old town of Conisbrough
were dark and silent as Robin tethered his horse
by the church and made his way to where he
could look across at the hill on which stood Earl
William's castle.

What he saw made his stomach go cold, for
the arched gateway of the castle was flanked by
two round towers, and on either side were high
walls that ran from tower to tower in a ring that
encircled the hilltop. Rising above the walls was
the tallest keep-tower he had ever seen. In the
moonlight it had the look of a smooth pillar of
stone, and the chinks of light that showed
through the shuttered slits of its windows
seemed as far out of reach as the stars in the
night sky.

"So Will was right," said Robin to himself. "I

can see now why Little John turned away in despair."

Behind him he heard a calling of farewells, and looking round he saw a burly man in a friar's robes swaying out of the doorway of a tavern. The friar walked over to a washing-trough, splashed his face heartily, then straightened and stretched and looked curiously at Robin.

"A blessing on you, good sir," said the friar. "Has something of note happened in the sky tonight, or do you make a habit of standing around gazing at the moon?"

"I was gazing at Earl William's castle," answered Robin. "There is a maiden within those walls I wish to meet."

The friar nodded gravely. "I have often wondered," he said, "why the wickedest of knights should have the fairest of the maidens – not, of course, that it is any real concern of a holy man like myself. I fear you would be well advised to forget this maiden of yours."

"Are the castle gates never open to strangers?" asked Robin.

"Only on Sundays," replied the friar. "The earl is so proud of his new chapel that he likes to fill it with worshippers, though even then I imagine you would need to be a richly-dressed knight to be allowed through its door."

"Well, I thank you for your advice," said Robin.

"You are most welcome," replied the friar. "If you wish to repay me, remember me in your prayers. I need all the help I can get."

Robin rode out of Conisbrough by a road that led not to the forest, but to the village where he had been born. He was soon riding with lowered eyes past the fields that had been his in the days before he was outlawed, and he tethered

his horse in the woods behind the house of Sir
Gilbert Fitzwalter.

As he stepped into Sir Gilbert's orchard, he
saw a huge wolfhound loping towards him with
its ears pricked up in suspicion. Robin knelt
down and beckoned to it.

"Come now, Sigurd, you old monster," he

called softly. "Surely you remember me?" The wolfhound leapt forward, and a moment later had its paws on Robin's shoulders and was licking his face.

"Now," said Robin, "let us see if we can find a way of letting Marian know I am here without waking the whole household."

It was not long after midsummer, and the apples on the trees were still young and green. Robin twisted one from its branch and threw it so that it thumped against the shutters of Marian's chamber, and as he did so he hooted like an owl. To make an echo he threw a second apple, with a second owl's call to keep it company.

Before long the door of the house was edged open, and Marian came running towards him through the moonlight. Over her shift of white linen she had pinned a mantle embroidered with flowers, but Robin barely noticed, for his eyes went to her face. His arms stretched out towards her, and as he clasped her tight he was the happiest man in all Christendom.

When they had spoken words of love, and poured out the longing for each other that they carried in their hearts, Robin told her of Little

John and of the maiden imprisoned in the castle of Conisbrough.

"The answer is clear," said Marian. "To pass through the gates of Conisbrough you will have to become a knight."

Robin laughed and kissed her. "And where, my love," he asked, "am I to find a coat of chain-mail and all the other finery that go to make a knight?"

"Perhaps," said Marian, "you could borrow them from a man who is now our most eager visitor, Sir Guy of Gisburn."

"Is this true?" asked Robin, looking around as if the house had become tainted. "Sir Guy comes here?"

"He thinks we are his friends," replied Marian. "Ever since the day we tricked him in Pontefract, he believes that my father and I have the same hatred for you in our hearts that he carries in his own. I am happy he should think so, for whenever he is here with us I know that you are safe."

"Still, I do not see how that can help," said Robin.

"You and Sir Guy are of much the same build," said Marian. "If you were to shave off your beard, then crop your hair short the way he wears his, then ride up to Conisbrough wearing his chain-mail and colours…"

"My love," said Robin, "your wits are sharper than the east wind."

"Let me tell him that your mother has brought us a message that you wish to meet with him," suggested Marian. "Where shall I say you wish the meeting to be?"

Robin thought for a moment, then broke into a smile.

"At Wentbridge," he answered, "on the high-road, where there is a grange of white monks. There could be no better place."

4 Trickery at Wentbridge

So it came about that on the following Sunday, Sir Guy of Gisburn left Pontefract before daybreak, riding at the head of a dozen men-at-arms too sleepy to grumble at the way they had been ordered from their beds.

Riding beside Sir Guy was his sergeant-at-arms, a grim old warrior by the name of Serlo.

"Where are we bound?" he asked Sir Guy.

"To Wentbridge," replied the knight. "The outlaw Robin Hood has sent word that he wishes to meet with me."

"It has the smell of a trap," said Serlo.

"Indeed," agreed Sir Guy, "which is why I wish to get there early, and set a trap of my own."

"What do you have in mind?" asked the sergeant.

"Something sweet and simple," said Sir Guy. "I want you and the men to hide in the woods with your crossbows at the ready, and when Robin Hood shows himself, I want you to shoot him as full of arrows as if he were Saint Sebastian."

"That sounds simple enough," agreed Serlo. "Leave it to us."

In the damp summer dawn they reached the rim of a wooded valley, and found themselves looking down on the village of Wentbridge. At a nod from Sir Guy, Serlo led the men-at-arms off the road into the trees, and the knight rode on down the hill alone.

When he reached the bridge he dismounted, and turning his horse loose to graze in the meadows, he leaned against the parapet and let his eyes rove over the village. He knew the place well. To one side of the road lay the walled grange with its chapel and cluster of farm buildings, while on the other stood an inn and a few ramshackle houses. Despite the monks, Wentbridge had an evil name, and travellers never stopped there after dark; but in the gathering sunlight, with his men-at-arms hidden in the woods at his back, Sir Guy felt as bold as a lion.

Almost at once he saw a man emerge from the gateway of the grange and come walking towards him. He wore a forester's tunic of Lincoln green, but his face was clean-shaven and his hair cropped short, and in no way did he look like a man of the woods. It was by the sword hanging from his belt, a sword the knight had once seen drawn against him, that Sir Guy knew his man.

"Well met, Robin Hood," he said calmly.

"Well met, Sir Guy," replied Robin, coming to a halt twenty paces away, at the far end of the bridge.

"You make a fine target," said Sir Guy with a smile.

"So do you," answered Robin.

The smile withered on Sir Guy's lips as a second man dressed in green stepped out from under the trailing branches of a willow tree by the water's edge. He carried a longbow, with an arrow notched to the string, and as he walked forward he raised the bow so that the arrow pointed straight at Sir Guy's throat.

"You may remember my friend, Will Scarlet," said Robin. "Take my word for it that he never misses his mark."

Sir Guy waited until the outlaws were standing side by side at the far end of the bridge, then he threw himself to the ground.

"Shoot them both!" he yelled.

Nothing happened. No crossbow bolts hissed through the air to break the calm of the summer morning, and before Sir Guy could save himself, Robin had leapt on top of him and drawn the knight's sword from his scabbard. A moment later Sir Guy was being tickled under the chin by the tip of his own sword-blade.

"Now, Sir Guy," said Robin, "you may rise very slowly to your feet. One rash move and your head goes flying into the river."

The knight could do nothing but obey, and as he stood up he shuddered with the same cold fear that he had spent his life inflicting on others. Looking round he saw his men-at-arms, stripped of their weapons, being chased out of the woods by a band of monks. At first he could hardly believe his eyes, but when he blinked and looked again he saw that the monks were bearded and carried longbows. One of them was so huge that his monk's habit barely came down to his knees.

"What devilry is this?" asked Sir Guy.

"I would call it a miracle," said Robin Hood.

76

"We asked the monks for the loan of their clothes, then locked them into their chapel. When we left them they were saying their prayers as if nothing had happened."

The men-at-arms were herded onto the bridge, and Sir Guy came face to face with Serlo, who smiled sourly.

"Have you anything to say for yourself?" Sir Guy asked him.

"Not a lot," answered Serlo. "One moment we heard monks walking down the road singing a psalm, and the next we were surrounded by wild men with longbows."

"Get these pigs into the grange," shouted Robin. "Much and Dickon, run back up the hill and get their horses."

Once inside the grange, Sir Guy and his men were prodded and poked into a corner of the courtyard. The outlaws shaped themselves into a line, and their arrows were still notched to their bows.

"Now," said Robin, "I want you to strip to your shirts, and to throw your clothes and armour into a heap."

"You can burn in hell first," retorted Sir Guy.

"I fear you would get there before me," said

...obin, "but I have no time to argue. We can always take the clothes from your dead bodies, if that is how you wish it to be."

The outlaws raised their bows and took aim.

"What do we do?" Serlo asked his master.

Sir Guy looked thoughtfully at the outlaws, and the one who impressed him most was as tall as a giant and grinning from ear to ear, as if he could hardly wait to loose his arrow.

"We do whatever they want," muttered Sir Guy.

Helmets and belts, metal-ringed hauberks and boots and hose: all were pulled off and thrown into a heap, until Sir Guy and his men stood barefoot in their shirts. The outlaws roared with laughter, and Robin unbolted the heavy door of one of the farm buildings and swung it open.

"We can hardly let you wander the roads unarmed," said Robin. "You would be quite at the mercy of the wicked robbers who live in the forest. So for your own protection we will shut you up in here with the other swine."

Before Sir Guy could protest he was flung into a dark and stinking barn. His men were pushed in on top of him, and as the door was slammed and bolted, they slithered around and fell over each other. Hogs bit their ankles in the blackness, and

as soon as he found his way back to what felt like
the door, Sir Guy hammered on it with his fists.

"I swear you will pay for this," he shouted. "Do
you hear me, Robin Hood? Do you hear me?"

But there was no reply.

5 The Dark Tower

As the bells summoning the faithful to Mass rang
out over the castle and town of Conisbrough, a
group of horsemen drew rein on the edge of the
town. Anyone who saw them from afar would
have taken them for Sir Guy of Gisburn and his
men-at-arms.

Sweating inside Sir Guy's helmet like a mop in
a bucket, Robin turned to his companions.

"This is as far as we ride together," he told
them. "Little John will come with me into the
castle. The rest of you must wait in the town. If I
blow on my horn, make for the gateway, for it
means we are in trouble, and if we get out in one
piece we will need you there to shoot down who-
ever is hard on our heels."

Will Scarlet rolled his eyes to heaven. "May
luck go with you," he said miserably.

Robin Hood and Little John rode on through the town and took the track that climbed towards the castle gateway.

"It is strange how the walls look higher in daylight," said Robin.

"I may not even reach them," muttered Little John. "This coat of chain-mail is killing me."

"We are almost there," said Robin. "Try to look proud and magnificent."

The hooves of their horses clattered onto the timbers of the drawbridge.

"Make way for Sir Guy of Gisburn!" cried Little John, and the guards in the shadows of the gateway took one look at their finery and stood back to let them pass.

As they entered the castle-yard they saw it was crowded with horses and wagons and servants rushing to and fro. Robin beckoned with a knightly gloved hand to a boy who was on his way to the kitchens with a rack of hares.

"Tell me," he said haughtily, "why are there so many people here today?"

"Earl William returned last night," answered the boy as he hurried past.

"Saints preserve us," said Little John. "He never travels with less than eighty men-at-arms."

"That could be a blessing in disguise," said Robin. "Ernald of Mort may hardly notice two more strangers. We have timed it well. It seems they are all in the chapel." As they dismounted he gazed around the halls that stood against the battlements. "Where do we look for your maiden?" he asked. "She could be in any one of a hundred chambers."

"Meg says that Ernald keeps her shut up in the keep," said Little John.

Robin spun round. "Who is Meg?" he asked, but Little John was already striding across the castle-yard towards the thick, high tower that looked a fortress in itself.

The doorway of the tower was high above the ground, and they climbed to it by a narrow stair of stone. Little John twisted the iron ring of the door handle and gave a snarl of dismay.

"Locked," he said.

"Locked from outside," said Robin, "which means that it is closed by a single bolt. If we could only break the bolt..."

"With God's help it will be done," said Little John.

They waited until a sound of chanting came from the chapel, then Little John stood back and

began to breathe fast and deep. His nostrils flared, his fists clenched, and the veins stood out on his wrists. At the seventh breath he stepped forward, kicking high with his right leg, and brought his foot slamming down on the lock. The oaken door shuddered, and with a splintering of wood it swung open, while the lock, smashed from its frame, dropped with a clink into the yard.

"This is truly a day of miracles," said Robin.

They found themselves in a dark and empty

chamber, and turned at once to follow a stair-passage that twisted up through the thick stone walls. Narrow shafts of light came slanting in through the windows, but there were so few windows that it seemed as if they were climbing into a tomb. The passage led them to a second chamber, where again there was no one to be seen, and they hurried on up the stairs into the chamber above.

There, as they entered, they heard prayers being spoken by two soft voices. Set into the walls of the tower was a small vaulted chapel, and

kneeling by the altar were a woman in simple clothes and a maiden with long braided hair and a face as pale as snow. Little John tore the helmet from his head.

"Have no fear, Meg," he said. "It is only me."

"John," exclaimed the woman, clapping her hands to her face. Robin turned to meet the widening blue eyes of the maiden.

"You must be the lady Clara," he said with a smile. "John did not tell me of your beauty."

"This is my good friend Robin Hood," said Little John. "We have come to take you away from here."

"It may be," said Robin, "if we hurry."

He led them quickly down through the tower and out into the sunlight of the castle-yard. As they walked towards the horses, the doors of the chapel were thrown open, and out spilled a crowd of over a hundred knights and ladies and men-at-arms.

"Too late," said Little John. "We are trapped."

"Not yet," said Robin, and he spoke under his breath to Meg and Clara. "Keep walking towards the horses..."

"Who goes there?" cried a voice from the crowd, and its owner was a knight with a swarthy face who came striding towards them.

"I am Guy of Gisburn," cried Robin, "and I challenge you to combat, Ernald of Mort, in the name of the maiden you have so cruelly imprisoned."

A second knight, who Robin guessed to be Earl William, came hurrying forward. "What is the meaning of this?" he demanded. "No maiden has ever been wronged in my castle."

"Sir Ernald has betrayed your trust, my lord earl," said Robin.

Sir Ernald's eyes narrowed into slits in a mask of anger. "Men to arms!" he yelled. "Seize the intruders! Bar the gate!"

Yet even as he spoke, the air hissed and it was as if the sky filled with serpents of smoke. Over their heads flew ten burning arrows, to thud one after another into the roof of the chapel. Around their shafts were tied rags soaked in pitch, which splashed over the roof-timbers like golden rain. Robin looked up to see Will Scarlet and one of the outlaws standing on a tower high above the gateway, loosing a second volley of arrows towards a hall on the other side of the yard. The air filled with smoke.

"Fire!" screamed Earl William. "Fetch water!

Save my chapel!"

Men ran in all directions, and only Ernald of Mort stood his ground. He looked from the chapel roof to the archers on the battlements, then at Robin, and made to draw his sword. Before his hand could clasp the hilt he caught a blow from a giant fist that knocked him straight out of the daylight into night.

Little John rubbed his knuckles and turned to Robin. "Shall we take our leave?" he asked.

"It would certainly be wrong to overstay our

welcome," agreed Robin.

Meg and Clara were ready with the horses, and a moment later the four of them were riding through the gateway where the guards had been tied up like turkeys. Will and the outlaws came running down the stairway from the tower and followed them out, and on the far side of the drawbridge they met Much and Dickon puffing up the hill dragging a wagon filled with kindling, which in no time at all had been pushed into the gateway and set alight.

"That should keep the wasps in their nest for a while," said Will Scarlet. "Well done, lads."

"What were you doing up on the battlements?" Robin asked him. "I thought I told you to wait in the town?"

Will scratched his chin. "Perhaps you did," he said. "My memory is not what it used to be."

"I hope you remember where you left your horses," said Robin.

And anyone who saw them from afar would have thought that Sir Guy of Gisburn and his men-at-arms were leaving Conisbrough in something of a hurry.

6 Hearts of the Forest

But Sir Guy of Gisburn and his men-at-arms were still locked in the pigsty of the monks of Wentbridge, and they were not in good cheer. Hours had gone by, and they were beginning to learn what it was like to be shut away in a dungeon and forgotten.

"If ever we escape from here, " said one of them, "I vow never again to push men into prison."

"And I vow to give all I have stolen back to the poor," said another.

"Quiet, you fools," ordered Sir Guy. "Something is happening outside."

In the courtyard they heard a milling of horses, and the sound of voices raised in laughter. Sir Guy hammered on the door with his fists, but no one paid him any heed, and they were still locked in darkness when silence returned to the grange.

Another long hour had passed when finally the door was unbolted and opened by a white-haired monk who gasped at the sight of the prisoners.

"By Saint Bridget!" he cried. "A miracle! Our hogs are turning human!"

Sir Guy pushed past him and staggered out into the sunlight, followed by his muck-spattered men. Heaped in the centre of the yard they saw their clothes and armour.

"Where are our horses?" Sir Guy asked the monk.

"Horses? Ah, horses," murmured the monk, who was Brother Hubert. "I seem to remember seeing some horses grazing in the meadows by the river."

As soon as they had rummaged their way back into their clothes, Sir Guy led his men in search of their mounts. They were gathering them together when a cavalcade of knights came thundering down the road and galloped into the meadow to surround them.

"Throw down your weapons, Guy of Gisburn," ordered a knight, "and tell us where you have hidden the lady Clara."

"The lady Clara?" repeated Sir Guy. "I know no one of that name."

"We are in no mood to play games," replied the knight, and he signalled to his followers.

"Tie them to their horses," he ordered. "They will speak soon enough under torture."

Nothing the men from Pontefract could say made any difference. They were dragged to the castle of Conisbrough and thrown at the feet of Earl William and Ernald of Mort.

"Have mercy, my lords," begged Sir Guy. "This is all a mistake."

"Are you not Guy of Gisburn?" asked Earl William.

"Yes," answered Sir Guy, "but I am not the man you seek."

Earl William sniffed at his prisoner. "It is true you do not smell like a knight," he admitted. "What do you have to say for yourself?"

So Sir Guy saved himself from torture, but only by telling the story of how he had been tricked out of his clothes by the outlaw Robin Hood. It was a story that travelled fast, and for a long time afterwards Sir Guy could go nowhere without hearing the sound of muffled laughter behind his back.

While all this was happening, Robin Hood and his companions came safely to their lair in the depths of the forest of Barnsdale. Waiting for them there were Marian and the young knight Adam, whom she had sought out in Melton, and found brooding over the maiden he thought he had lost forever.

At the sight of her true love, Clara gave a cry of delight, and jumped from her horse into his arms. Nor was Robin any slower in running to Marian.

"My love," said Robin, "your beauty lights up in the forest. Will the day never come that you join us here?"

"The day will surely come," said Marian, "when I can stay away no longer; but in the meantime, you must come more often to pick the apples in my orchard."

They turned to see Clara and Adam standing before them.

"How can I thank you, Robin Hood?" asked Clara.

"Why only me?" asked Robin. "Thank John for leading me to you. Thank Marian for finding the ruse to get us through the gates. Thank Will and the brotherhood for saving our lives."

"I thank you all," cried Clara. "If there is any way I can help you, you have only to say."

"You can help us by finding safety," replied Robin. "Do either of you have family who live beyond the reach of Ernald of Mort?"

"My father has lands in Cumbria," said Adam. "He will give us shield and shelter."

"Then you must travel there by lonely roads," said Robin. "Will Meg go with you?"

"She is my much loved nurse," answered Clara. "I would not dream of leaving her behind."

Out of the corner of his eye, Robin had seen Meg take Little John by the hand.

"You are a good man, John," said Meg. "Will you come with us?"

"Oh, my road lies elsewhere," said Little John, and Robin could see that it tore his heart to say it.

"We must be leaving," said Marian to the young ones. "I will set you on your road."

Meg nodded sadly, then stretched up on tiptoe to give Little John a kiss, and the giant turned as red as a berry.

When the farewells had been spoken, the out-laws watched their friends ride away through the forest. Little John stood like a man unsure what to do next, and Robin reached up and set his hand on the giant's shoulder.

"Little John," he said, "from all I have seen I would say your heart is in the right place."

"So is yours," answered the giant.

"Then will you sup with us," asked Robin, "before you take your road to the Holy Land?"

Little John folded his arms and glowered.

"Are you suggesting," he asked, "that I should go flying off like a swan when there is plainly some hard work to be done around here?"

"Never," said Robin, and he held out his hand.

Little John grinned and clasped it in a giant's grip that made Robin yell with pain.

"By my faith," cried Robin. "You could crush a stone. I may never be able to draw my bow again."

But he did, and often, and Little John was always there to follow it with an arrow of his own. All the outlaws of the brotherhood felt stronger with a giant in their midst, but out of all the bonds of love and trust that were forged by their adventures, no two friends grew closer than did Robin Hood and Little John.